Case of The Christmas Concert Catastrophe

By Kyla Steinkraus

Illustrated by David Ouro

Rourke
Educational Media
rourkeeducationalmedia.com

www.rourkeeducationalmedia.com

Edited by: Keli Sipperley
Cover and Interior layout by: Renee Brady
Cover and Interior Illustrations by: David Ouro

Library of Congress PCN Data

Case of the Christmas Concert Catastrophe / Kyla Steinkraus
(Rourke's Mystery Chapter Books)
ISBN (hard cover)(alk. paper) 978-1-63430-379-8
ISBN (soft cover) 978-1-63430-479-5
ISBN (e-Book) 978-1-63430-574-7
Library of Congress Control Number: 2015933735

Printed in China, FACE Worldwide Limited,
Kowloon, Hong Kong

Dear Parents and Teachers:

With twists and turns and red herrings, readers will enjoy the challenge of Rourke's Mystery Chapter Books. This series set at Watson Elementary School builds a cast of characters that readers quickly feel connected to. Embedded in each mystery are experiences that readers encounter at home or school. Topics of friendship, family, and growing up are featured within each book.

Mysteries open many doors for young readers and turn them into lifelong readers because they can't wait to find out what happens next. Readers build comprehension strategies by searching out clues through close reading in order to solve the mystery.

This genre spreads across many areas of study including history, science, and math. Exploring these topics through mysteries is a great way to engage readers in another area of interest. Reading mysteries relies on looking for patterns and decoding clues that help in learning math skills.

Whether readers are reading the books independently or you are reading with them, engaging with them after they have read the book is still important. We've included several activities at the end of each book to make this both fun and educational.

Do you think you and your reader have what it takes to be a detective? Can you solve the mystery? Will you accept the challenge?

Rourke Educational Media

Table of Contents

Snow Day

It was only Monday morning, but I already knew it was going to be an awesome week. When I woke up and looked out the window next to my bed, the whole entire backyard was white! The ground was white, Panda's doghouse was white, and every branch of my backyard maple tree glistened white like they'd been frosted with icing.

On a regular day, I would have snuggled in with Panda and stared at the snow until Mom had to threaten me with missing breakfast.

"Today is not a regular day," I said to Panda as I brushed my hair and tugged on my boots at the same time. Okay, it didn't work so well. I fell flat on my bottom. Plus, I'd forgotten socks. Oops.

Panda didn't mind. He licked my face. I'm from China. Panda bears are from China, too. Even though Panda wasn't technically a bear, he was the next best thing.

I rushed through the rest of my getting-ready jobs and was out the door a whole seven minutes early.

"That was pretty much a world record, Lyra Liang!" Mom said as she kissed me goodbye.

On the way to school, Dad quizzed me on my spelling words: appetite, believe, perhaps, excel. Most of them were pretty easy, but I kept forgetting excel has only one L.

"I just can't concentrate on school stuff right now, Dad."

"Oh, right. The big audition results. How could I forget?"

Watson Elementary's Christmas concert was less than three weeks away. Our music teacher, Mrs. Center, held auditions last Friday for the three solo parts. She'd promised to post the results on the bulletin board today.

"Are you nervous?"

I had a funny feeling in my stomach like dragonflies were zooming around in there.

"More like super excited. This is my year, Dad.

You're gonna be so proud," I said. Dad laughed as we pulled into the school drop-off lane.

"I have a feeling you're going to knock it out of the park," he said.

I leaned over the front seat and kissed him on the cheek.

"I don't even know what that means! See you soon, racoon."

"Take care, polar bear," he said. I ran up the sidewalk. The custodian, Mr. Doyle, was spreading salt everywhere to melt the icy snow, while Mr. Sleuth, the school secretary, shoveled the sidewalk.

Mr. Sleuth was nice and also tremendously tall. Probably even taller than a giraffe. I waved up at him.

"Hi there, Lyra." He waved down at me.

I waved again and opened the front door. The school principal, Mrs. Holmes, stood in the lobby. Mrs. Holmes was super short for a grownup, but she made up for it in special principal powers.

"Good morning, Lyra," she said.

"Mr. Sleuth is wearing bright pink ear muffs,"

I said.

"Is he now?" Mrs. Holmes said with a grin.

Just then two of my best friends rushed in, Caleb James and Alex Price.

"I'm a snow monster!" Caleb yelled, kicking snow from his boots all over the carpet.

"Hurry on to class, kids," Mrs. Holmes said.

"Race you!" Caleb said, but Mrs. Holmes turned the Holmes Eye on him. The Holmes Eye was like a laser that could see all the not-so-good things you'd done that day, or maybe even for your whole life.

Caleb's face turned red as a tomato. He cleared his throat. "I mean, walk you!"

We tiptoed all the way to homeroom, room 113, the best third-grade classroom in the history of Watson Elementary.

The Gumshoe Gang

Tully Johnson and Ronald "Rocket" Gonzaga were already in their seats. The desks were clustered together in groups of five. I sat with Tully, Rocket, Caleb, and Alex, my four best friends in the whole world.

Ever since we cracked the case of the missing crystal statue way back in second grade, we'd been inseparable, both as best friends and as ace detectives. We were even known as the Gumshoe Gang. At first I thought I really had gum stuck to my shoe, but a gumshoe is a nickname for a detective, someone who investigates mysteries. Being a gumshoe is nearly as much fun as singing.

I am pretty good at a lot of things, but my best thing is singing. Okay, also talking too much.

Just then something smacked my head.

"Hey!"

"Oops, sorry." Rocket was tossing crumpled up paper balls into the trash can by the door. "One of my Megastar Asteroids must've lost its way."

I rolled my eyes. Rocket got his name from being speedy fast. He was best at sports and just being goofy.

"Nice try," I said.

"Hi, Lyra," Tully said. "Any news?" Tully was the most stylish detective in the universe. Today she wore neon yellow leggings paired with a glittery blue tutu and a purple sweater dotted with green hearts.

"No." I sighed. "I'll probably have to wait the whole entire day to find out."

"You aren't actually worried, are you?" Alex asked. Alex was best at science and finding clues. He was even smarter than some of the fifth graders.

"Well, only kind of," I admitted. "I just want to know for sure!"

"Everyone knows you're gonna get it," Caleb said. "Hey, does anyone have a pencil?" He dug around inside his disaster of a desk. Caleb's best things were math and being funny. Also, he was the messiest kid in the whole school.

Tully handed him a pink pencil with a unicorn eraser. "Want to help in Mrs. Center's room after school today, Lyra?"

Mrs. Center was letting the students make all the concert decorations: giant blue, white, and silver snowflakes to hang from the gym ceiling and pin to the walls, life-size cardboard Christmas trees, and a huge painted backdrop of snowcapped mountains and a wintry forest. The concert theme was Winter Wonderland.

I tucked my short black hair behind my ears and shook my head. "No, sorry. Mom said I have to give Panda a bath. And study my spelling."

"Good morning, class!" Our homeroom teacher, Miss Flores, took off her gray knit hat and shook out her dark curly hair. Miss Flores was about the nicest, prettiest teacher Watson Elementary ever had. Her name even meant flower in Spanish.

"Good morning, Miss Flores!" we echoed.

"Are we ready to play Favorite Things?"

We gathered around the learning rug, a big brown shaggy rug with white circles on it. I sat next to my friend Javier on one side and a girl with bright red hair and freckles named Abby on the other. Favorite Things was one of my favorite things! I raised my hand up high in the air.

Miss Flores picked Caleb first.

"I had my favorite meal of macaroni and cheese last night," he said.

"My favorite thing for today will be playing in the snow at recess," Xavier said.

I wiggled my fingers but Miss Flores chose Addison, and then her twin brother Aidan, who were both excited about the brownies packed in their lunches.

I stretched my arm until my shoulder popped right out of its socket. Not really, but it sure felt like it. Miss Flores still picked somebody else. Abby said, "My favorite thing today is music class because today is—"

"Today is AUDITION RESULTS day!" I yelled. I clapped my hand over my mouth. Oops.

Miss Flores frowned.

"Lyra, remember what we discussed about keeping our lips zipped when other people are talking. That's two tickets. You can give them to me at the end of the day."

My stomach did a yucky flip-flop.

"I'm sorry," I whispered.

"Apology accepted," Abby said.

Miss Flores smiled at Abby.

"Go ahead. What were you saying?"

"I tried out for the solo. I thought, I was hoping I might get it — "

"But *I'm* singing the solo," I interrupted. "Because I'm the best singer in the whole third grade!"

That was how I ended up missing all of first recess. I slumped in the Thinking Chair while my friends built snowmen and had snowball fights. My dumb mouth always got me into trouble. I wish I didn't have a mouth, so then there'd be no trouble. But then, no singing. Ugh.

Solo Achievement

Between–and also during–science, spelling, language arts, and reading, I used the drinking fountain at least two dozen times, which meant I also had to use the bathroom a bunch, which meant Miss Flores had lots of frustration in her voice by the end of the day. Every time I checked, the bulletin board held the same old stuff: announcements for tutoring, the lunch menu, and a note from Mrs. Holmes to please remember drinking fountains are for drinking, not for splashing water on your friends.

When the last bell rang, I raced to the bulletin board along with every other student in the entire third, fourth, and fifth grades.

"Come on!" Tully grabbed my hand. Together we nudged our way through the crowd.

The concert solo list was posted! I jumped up

and down to see over the big kids' heads. Some kids cheered but most groaned. I couldn't quite make it out. Were there two names for third grade?

"You got it, Lyra!" Tully yelled. Yes! I felt like a beautiful balloon getting bigger and bigger with all the happiness filling up inside me.

"Way to go, Lyra!" Rocket's sister Joy said.

"Can't wait to hear you sing," Joy's friend Dalia said. My cheeks got red from all the attention.

"Thank you. Did you get one too?"

"I did," Joy said. "I'm going to play my harp."

"I didn't!" A boy with spiky yellow hair and black-framed glasses snapped. "I took those stupid singing lessons all year for nothing. I deserved it more than anybody, even you, Joy!" He shoved past me and Tully and stalked off down the hallway.

"Why's he mad at me?" Joy asked. She blinked fast and her eyes were shiny like she was trying to keep tears from coming out. Caleb tapped her arm.

"Don't let him step on your thunder, Joy," Caleb said.

Dalia made a how-dumb-can-you-be face at Caleb and put her arm around Joy's shoulder.

"Don't worry about Travis. I'll talk to him." They walked up the stairs toward the fifth-grade classrooms.

"Hey! Lyra's not the only name on here," Tully said, gesturing at the bulletin board. "It says the solo will be shared. Abby won too!"

I was so surprised I could have fallen right over. I didn't even know Abby could sing! And just like that, the beautiful floaty balloon inside me popped, and all the happiness deflated right out.

"Abby!" Caleb yelled as we ran up to her. Tully told Abby she would be singing a solo too.

"Oh, wow! That's great," she said, but her voice was squeaky. Her skin was white as paper underneath her freckles.

"Are you okay?" Tully asked.

Abby blinked. She smiled, but it was sorta lopsided, like it might slide right off her face. "I'm just nervous, I guess."

"There's nothing to be nervous about," I snapped. My stomach did that painful twisty thing, like it was full of really angry snakes. "At least, not if you're the best singer in third grade, like me."

Mr. Sleuth began announcing the parents waiting in the pick-up line. " . . . Alex Price, time to go . . . Rocket and Joy Gonzaga, your chariot awaits . . ."

"That wasn't so nice," Tully whispered as we gathered our things.

"I know." I sighed. I slung my backpack over

my shoulder and trudged down the hallway. My legs felt heavier with every step. I got the solo I wanted. So why did I feel so bad?

For the next four days, it wasn't hard to keep my lips zipped. I was quiet as an unhappy mouse. In music, I practiced the song I shared with Abby, "Silent Night," but it was going so awful that Mrs. Center kept making us start over again.

In math, we took a multiplication test, but I couldn't concentrate and got most of it circled with red pen. In computer lab, we practiced typing our spelling words in different sentences. I couldn't think of any good sentences, so the computer teacher, Mrs. Collywobbles, gave me homework. Yuck. In art, we worked on dozens of giant snowflakes, drawing them, cutting them out, and painting them with glittery silver and white paint. That part wasn't so bad.

Every day the sky kept snowing and snowing. Outside was nothing but yuck — cold, wet, and gloomy. Exactly what my insides felt like. Miss Flores and Mrs. Center and all of my friends were happy for Abby, so I tried to be happy too.

Okay, I didn't really. Not even a little.

A Very Cold Case

It was Friday afternoon when something so big happened I almost totally forgot about all my problems. Lunch was finished, and we were strolling into the art and music room.

"My snowflakes are gone!" Javier cried. He stood in the corner with his hands on his hips, staring at where we'd stacked the in-progress decorations. The poster board, paints, paintbrushes, string, and scissors were piled neatly in front of the plywood backdrop. But everyone's snowflakes had disappeared!

"Oh dear, oh dear," Mrs. Center murmured, tugging on one of her dangly earrings. "I've been on the music side of the classroom all morning and didn't even notice. Who was here after school yesterday?"

Tully, Abby, and Javier raised their hands.

"Joy and Dalia were here too," Abby said. "When I left, everything was fine."

"Maybe someone moved them," Mrs. Center said, but she didn't sound too sure. We searched everywhere, even behind Mrs. Center's desk, inside the dusty art closet, and under the piano.

"It's like looking for a needle in a hayride!" Caleb said, peeking under a basket of paintbrushes.

There was not a single snowflake anywhere. At least, not inside. I glanced out the window at the whirling snow. The storage shed roof was covered, and the metal fence looked like it was wrapped in a fluffy white scarf.

"Who stole my snowflakes?" Javier wailed. His face got all scrunched up and red. "Whoever did it, I'm gonna sic Godzilla the Great on you! And he's gonna bite your bottom off!"

Everybody knew Godzilla the Great was a teeny tiny wiener dog, and the worst thing he could bite was ankles. But nobody reminded Javier of that. We were all feeling just as sad and angry as he was.

Mrs. Center patted Javier's shoulder. "I'm sure there's a good explanation for this."

"I have an idea," Rocket said. "Maybe aliens zapped them into their spaceship because they wanted to study snow that wouldn't melt."

Aidan raised his hand.

"Maybe cardboard-eating monsters broke into the school in the middle of the night and had a delicious meal chewing our snowflakes to bits!"

"Or maybe Mr. Doyle moved them," Alex said. "He was cleaning in here yesterday; all the paper scraps are swept up underneath the art tables."

"That's a great suggestion, Alex," Mrs. Center said. "Would you guys like to go ask him?"

By "guys," she of course meant the Gumshoe Gang. And we of course said yes. Mrs. Center wrote out a hall pass and shooed us out of the room.

"How exciting! A new mystery!" Tully opened her locker and pulled out the most important book in the universe, a yellow polka-dotted notebook with REAL DETECTIVE CLUES: PRIVATE: NO PEEKING scrawled in purple marker across the front. And at the bottom: THAT MEANS YOU! It held all of the notes and ideas for our cases, from suspects and clues to alibis and motives.

"No jumping to conclusions," Alex said as we hurried down the empty hallway. "We need to talk to Mr. Doyle first."

Mr. Doyle's custodial closet and office were down in the basement, next to the cafeteria. Mr. Doyle was standing outside the closet, scowling as he tugged on a pair of gloves.

"You kids supposed to be down here?"

"Yes, sir," Alex said, showing him the hall pass. He explained about the missing snowflakes. "Did you take them from Mrs. Center's room?"

"Nope. Left 'em right where they were."

"Mr. Doyle," Tully said "has anybody been acting suspiciously?"

Mr. Doyle shook his head.

"Just the usual kids lurking about. How would I have time to notice anything when I'm hauling this rock salt around everywhere? Can't even keep it in my closet 'cause there's no room. I've got to traipse out to that storage shed five times a day because the blasted snow just won't stop. The shed door keeps banging around in the wind and hitting me in the head!"

Rocket snorted, but I kicked him in the shin. It was not polite to laugh at grownups.

"I'm sorry, Mr. Doyle," I said.

"Me too. I'm too old for this. Maybe it's time to retire somewhere with palm trees!"

"And volcanoes?" Rocket asked.

"No! Although, at least I'd be warm then, wouldn't I?"

"Do you think having no hair on your head means you lose heat faster than regular people?" Rocket asked.

Veins popped out on Mr. Doyle's big, shiny forehead. "What?" he said.

"Never mind him." Tully said. "You sure you didn't see anything else?"

"Eh." Mr. Doyle glared at Rocket, then shook his head. "Well, now that I'm thinking about it. There was this older boy hanging around outside the art and music room with his hands stuffed in his pockets, like he was up to no good."

"What did he look like?" I asked.

"Yellow hair. Black glasses. Now if you'll excuse me, I've got to spread all this salt before that doggone last bell rings."

We said goodbye and headed back. "He means Travis the Terrible," I said. "He was super angry he didn't get the solo."

Tully wrote Travis's name under a list titled *Suspects*.

"I saw him too. He was in the hall when my mom came to get me. I only stayed an hour because I had piano lessons."

"So he's our number one suspect," Caleb said.

"Our only suspect," I said.

Travis the Terrible

Mrs. Center really wanted to catch the crook who'd stolen her snowflakes, so she let us talk to Travis during class. We got to miss some of spelling, which was a major plus.

Travis leaned against the wall next to the drinking fountain. He crossed his arms over his chest and glared at us.

"What do you pipsqueaks want?" he growled.

I could hear the rest of the fifth grade practicing scales to warm up their voices: "Doh Re Mi Fa So La Ti Doh!" I hummed along. I couldn't help it. If school were just singing and painting all day, I'd get all A's for sure.

Tully explained the case.

"We wondered if you saw anything suspicious yesterday."

"No, nothing. Can I go now?" Travis said.

"Can you help us out first?" Tully asked. "Tell us everything you did yesterday. You might remember something important."

I wanted to shout, "Just admit it! We already know you did it!" But real live detectives are patient and careful and always one step ahead. That's how they catch the culprit. So I kept my lips zipped tight as a winter coat in a blizzard.

"Fine. Yesterday afternoon we had science lab, then library time, then math. After school I usually go to the extended day program until five."

"That's what you did?"

"No. I went to the art and music room to make decorations and stuff."

"That's a big fat lie!" I blurted. This lip zipping thing wasn't working so well.

"You're right. I didn't actually go." Travis cleared his throat a couple of times. He glanced down the hallway both ways like he was scared Godzilla was going to come roaring down the hall and eat him. Only not Javier's tiny dog, but the real Godzilla.

"I admit it, okay? I'm mad I didn't get that

singing part. I don't want to help with the dumb concert."

"Then why'd you go?" I asked.

Travis sighed.

"I wanted to talk to Joy, to tell her I was sorry for getting all mad at her. It wasn't her fault. But I wanted to talk to her alone, so I waited until she was done and came out."

"Oh," I said. That made sense. Too bad.

"Don't act so disappointed. I didn't take those stupid snowflakes. You can ask Joy. I walked back to extended day with her."

Tully jotted down a note.

"We'll check your alibi. Did you see anyone else?"

"Just that red-headed girl, the one who hardly talks. Also Javier and you." He tipped his chin towards Tully. "I saw Mr. Sleuth go into his office. Mr. Doyle was lugging salt around. Mrs. Collywobbles was flapping around the hall for a while, but I didn't see her go in the art and music room. That's it. Am I done?"

"I have an important question," Rocket said.

"How do you get your hair to stand up like that?"

"What's that got to do with anything?"

"Absolutely nothing," I said, glaring at Rocket. "You don't have to answer that."

"What did you mean by Mrs. Collywobbles 'flapping' around?" Alex asked.

Travis pushed himself away from the wall and uncrossed his arms. "Because of those big cloak things she's been wearing all winter. The sides are so loose and flappy, she looks like she has wings."

"A poncho." Tully closed the notebook.

"Yep, that thing. Now go away." Travis went back into the art and music room where the fifth graders were singing the first stanza of "Jingle Bell Rock."

"Do you think he's telling the truth?" I asked. He was awfully mean for a not-guilty person.

"Probably," Tully said. "We'll check with Joy, though. A detective must always follow through."

"We need to take another look at the crime scene, too," Alex said.

"Tully and I volunteer in the library after school today," I said. "But we could do it after that."

"I can go," Caleb said. "My mom has a haircut. She said she'd be done at 4:30 p.m. Come get me after the library. I'll go with you."

Classes inched along slower than a creepy crawly caterpillar. I knew I was feeling less bad because I lost five behavior tickets for too much talking.

After the last bell, Tully and I went to the library, where we got to take care of the librarian Mr. Hornswoggle's pets by cleaning out their cages and giving them fresh food and water. Cleaning cages was super gross, but playing with the pets afterward was the best part of Fridays.

After we finished, we found Caleb and went back to the art and music room. The halls were empty. Our boots made loud clomping sounds on the tile floor.

"It's kind of spooky all quiet like this," I whispered.

"Keep your eyes peeled for anything suspicious," Caleb whispered back.

Chapter Six

Clues in the Classroom

The art and music room door was shut, but it wasn't locked. Abby sat at a table, the sleeves of her purple sweater pushed back to her elbows. She was painting a big cardboard Christmas tree.

"Hey guys!" Her face was almost as red as her hair.

"It's colder than a penguin's bottom in here!" Caleb said.

Abby shrugged.

"Maybe the heater's broken," she said.

I looked around. "You're all by yourself?"

"Yep. I've been painting all afternoon. Joy and Dalia left a while ago. Mrs. Center went to an appointment. She said she'd be back to lock up the classroom around five."

Then I saw the backdrop. It was beautiful, with snowcapped mountains, glittering pine trees and

a blue sky. "Wow! Did you finish it?"

Abby nodded proudly.

Tully took out her pink rhinestone-studded magnifying glass and the three of us examined the room, checking the tables, the floor around the backdrop, the shelves and cabinets, and even the trash can. Trash cans were stinky and gross, but Alex told us to always check them for clues. This time, there wasn't anything but little colored bits of paper and some gum wrappers.

I went over to the window. Outside, millions of snowflakes swirled around in the wind. I shivered. "Brrr! It's freezing right here!"

"This window isn't shut all the way," Caleb said. He borrowed Tully's magnifying glass and studied the window. The sill was wet. There were also puddles on the floor under the art table and chairs.

"No wonder I was freezing," Abby said. "I even had to wear my coat for a while." She patted the damp wool coat hanging on the back of her chair.

Tully and I sat down across from Abby.

"Have you seen or heard anything unusual or

suspicious?"

Abby's face got red again. "Am I a suspect?" she sputtered.

"You're a witness. A witness is someone who sees something and tells the detectives about it so they can solve the case."

To a detective, everyone is a suspect. But I wasn't going to say that. This time my lips were really sealed.

Abby looked down at her hands.

"You talked to Travis already, right?" she asked. "I mean, other than him, Mrs. Center and Mrs. Collywobbles, there hasn't been anybody else around here."

"Mrs. Collywobbles the computer teacher?" I asked.

"Yeah, she's been here a bunch of times. She just walks in and looks around like she's searching for something. She sees me, waves hello, and then walks out. That's kinda weird, right?"

I looked at the clock. Oops. We were already late, so we said goodbye to Abby. I looped my arm through Tully's as we walked with Caleb toward the lobby. "You don't really think the crook is Mrs. Collywobbles, do you?"

"I sure hope not," Tully said.

"The concert is next Thursday." I squeezed Tully's arm, trying not to feel too worried. "We've got to get the snowflakes back by then."

"We'll burn that bridge when we come to it," Caleb said. He opened his locker and started to put the magnifying glass on the top shelf.

"No!" Tully and I yelled together.

Tully grabbed the magnifying glass just as two empty juice boxes, a pack of cards, and a mess of papers cascaded out of Caleb's locker. "Give it back to me. Otherwise we'll never see it again!"

"Oh, all right," Caleb said. "But you're both jinxed until Monday!"

Even though it was freezing cold outside, I felt all warm and fuzzy. No matter what happened, my friends were the best friends in the whole world.

A Turn for the Worse

On Monday morning, I kissed Panda goodbye and went to school with a skip in my step. The snowstorm was over and the sun shone in the bright blue sky.

At school, we'd just started to play Favorite Things on the learning rug when Mrs. Center burst into Room 113.

"Mrs. Center!" Miss Flores said in surprise. "Can we help you?"

"If you don't mind, could I borrow the Gumshoe Gang for a few moments?"

"We don't mind!" I said, jumping to my feet.

"Certainly." Miss Flores ushered us into the hallway. "Is everything okay?" she whispered to Mrs. Center.

Mrs. Center wiped at her eyes with her handkerchief.

"Oh, it's terrible. The concert backdrop— someone ruined it!"

"Oh no!" I gasped.

"They painted a big red X over the beautiful mountains and forest. Don't tell Abby yet, poor thing. She basically painted it all herself."

"When did this happen?" Tully asked, pulling her notebook out of the back pocket of her neon pink corduroy pants. "It was fine on Friday."

Mrs. Center blew her nose with her handkerchief.

"It's all my fault. I was planning to come back and lock the door at 5 p.m. after my appointment, but my errands ran late, and with the snow storm, I just didn't get back to the school."

Miss Flores hugged Mrs. Center. "I'm so sorry," she said.

"That's not even the worst thing," Mrs. Center blubbered. "They also took my sheet music and my conductor's baton. My father was an orchestra conductor. He gave it to me when I graduated from college. It's very special to me."

I took Mrs. Center's hand.

"Don't cry, Mrs. Center."

Mrs. Center sniffed a few times.

"Thank you, Lyra. Please catch him. If we don't find the decorations and my sheet music in time, the concert will have to be canceled."

This was terrible. If the concert was canceled, I wouldn't get to sing my solo, and I wouldn't get to stand in the big circle of light with everybody watching, and nobody would throw roses all over the stage. Everyone would be disappointed and sad and that would be the most awful thing to happen in the history of Watson Elementary. Also, it would completely ruin Christmas.

"We can't let that happen!"

"Don't worry," Caleb said. "We'll solve this case if it's the first thing we do."

After asking Mrs. Center a few more questions, we started down the hall.

"We should talk to Mr. Sleuth. He knows a lot about what's going on around here, especially with the grownups," Tully said, reading the case notes as she walked.

I knocked on the open door as we entered Mr.

Sleuth's office. "Hello?"

Mr. Sleuth sat behind his desk. He was so tall he made his desk look like a tiny kids' desk. He smiled broadly.

"Well, hello, Gumshoes. I hear you have a serious case to solve this morning."

"Yes, sir." I explained what Mr. Doyle, Travis, and Abby said about Mrs. Collywobbles.

"I agree this sounds concerning," Mr. Sleuth said. "I did indeed overhear a strange conversation between Mrs. Collywobbles and Miss Flores. It was last Thursday morning during recess when I was shoveling the snow around the benches. I only heard bits and pieces, but Mrs. Collywobbles declared she was leaving. She said Mrs. Center's name in a particularly nasty way. Miss Flores said something I didn't catch, and then Mrs. Collywobbles told Miss Flores that whatever she did, she must not tell anyone, or else! Then Mrs. Collywobbles noticed me nearby, and they ceased their clandestine conversation."

"Can you spell that?" Tully asked, writing furiously. "Clan—de-steen?"

Mr. Sleuth spelled the word: "C-L-A-N-D-E-S-T-I-N-E. It means secretive, undercover."

"I have an idea!" Rocket said. "Mrs. Collywobbles is an undercover alien! Her cover's been blown and now she must get out of dodge as quick as she can. But before she does, she needed to steal those snowflakes to take to the alien overlords."

"I'm not sure—" Tully began.

I nodded excitedly.

"Well, she's probably not an alien, but maybe she and Miss Flores are plotting revenge on Mrs. Center, which is why she's sabotaging the concert and stealing Mrs. Center's treasured possessions. And she sneaked out all the snowflakes under her ponchos!"

Tully smacked her own forehead. "Guys!" she said.

"Ace detective work!" Mr. Sleuth said, pounding on his desk with his fist.

Tully's eyes got big as golf balls, like she couldn't believe how awesome her friends were at solving mysteries. "Wait—what?"

Just then Mrs. Holmes opened her office door.

"What in the world is all the ruckus out here?"

"Oh, just cracking cases, Mrs. Holmes!" Mr. Sleuth leaned back in his chair and grinned.

"I'm all ears!" Mrs. Holmes said, but she didn't look too happy.

I explained our case, with Rocket adding his part about the aliens.

"Hmmm," Mrs. Holmes said when we finished. She closed her eyes and rubbed the side of her head. "Mrs. Collywobbles, would you join us?"

Mrs. Collywobbles walked through the doorway of Mrs. Holmes' office into Mr. Sleuth's office. She didn't look too happy, either.

"I think you received some misinformation," she said in an I'm-so-disappointed-in-you way.

My heart sank all the way down to my boots.

"Mr. Sleuth, when you were out on the playground shoveling, were you wearing your pink ear muffs?"

"Well, sure, I suppose I was."

I groaned.

"Then you couldn't have heard everything right, because your hearing was muffled."

Mr. Sleuth's face crumpled into a sad frown.

"Oh dear," he said.

"Oh dear isn't the half of it," Mrs. Holmes said sternly.

"Oh, it's all right, Mrs. Holmes," Mrs. Collywobbles said. "Surprisingly enough, Mr. Sleuth did hear a few things accurately. Plus, it is true that I have been acting different lately." Then Mrs. Collywobbles did her own surprising thing. She raised her arms and took her poncho off.

That's when my mouth dropped right open from shock. "Mrs. Collywobbles, you're ... that's a ..."

Rocket gasped. "You stole a basketball?!"

"No, silly. She's pregnant!" Tully said.

Mrs. Collywobbles laughed, and her round belly seemed to jiggle right along with her.

"Yes, I'm pregnant. With twins. And I will be leaving, but it's temporary, I promise. It's called maternity leave. I wasn't ready to tell everyone yet, so that's why I asked Miss Flores to keep it a secret. And of course, that's what the ponchos were for."

"What about all those times you went to Mrs. Center's classroom?" I asked.

"Mrs. Center is a good friend of mine. I've had terrible morning sickness with this pregnancy. Mrs. Center made a wonderful home remedy for me. I kept visiting her to get more."

Rocket steepled his fingers beneath his chin.

"And do your alien friends intend to analyze the crystalized structure and melting temperature of the snowflakes, or do they just like to eat cardboard?"

"Huh?" Mrs. Collywobbles asked, looking confused.

I sighed then said, "Never mind him."

"This is why you should never jump to conclusions," Mrs. Holmes said. "That's the first rule of detective work. Now, I believe you still have a case to solve, Gumshoes. There's not much time."

Then Mrs. Holmes turned the dreaded Holmes Eye on Mr. Sleuth. "Mr. Sleuth, may I have a word?"

Saving the Christmas Concert

We scurried out of the office as quick as we could. Out in the lobby, I asked Tully for her notebook. My heart felt like it was galloping a million miles a minute. I had an idea. A very big, possibly case-solving idea. I checked a few things and then looked up.

"I think I know who did it."

"Really? Who?" Caleb asked.

"First, we need our coats. Second, Mr. Doyle."

"Mr. Doyle's the thief?" Rocket asked incredulously.

"Just follow me." I led my friends downstairs. Mr. Doyle wasn't in his office, but we found him sweeping the girl's bathroom floor.

"We need your help," I told him.

Mr. Doyle put on his coat and took us outside. We walked single file, stepping into Mr. Doyle's footsteps as we followed him in the thick, crusted snow. We went around to the back of the school, stopping at the storage shed.

"We'll find our snowflakes in here," I said.

"I've been in here every day, and I haven't seen a thing," Mr. Doyle said, yanking open the shed door.

I was sure I was right. I walked past the shovels and the bags of rock salt and peered behind the big riding lawn mower. There they were: a hundred glittering blue, white, and silver snowflakes, plus a few cardboard Christmas trees. Mrs. Center's sheet music and her baton lay beside them on the concrete floor. Yes!

"Mrs. Center will be happier than a fox at a tea party!" Caleb exclaimed.

"It would've been totally cool if it really was aliens," Rocket said wistfully, stacking several snowflakes in his arms. We each carried as many snowflakes as we could and brought them back inside the school. Mr. Doyle spread them out on the stage in the gym to dry them out. Not a single one was ruined.

I smiled so big my cheeks hurt. "Now let's find our culprit." We went back to Mrs. Holmes' office. Mrs. Holmes listened to my story, and then called Mr. Sleuth to bring in the suspected student.

When she walked into the principal's office and saw the Gumshoe Gang, Abby's face went white. "Oh," she said in a small voice.

"Please sit down," Mrs. Holmes said gently.

Abby sat down. She gripped the arms of her chair, and she was shaking. I felt a pang in my stomach. Suddenly I felt sorry for Abby. She looked really scared.

"Abby Campbell, the Gumshoe Gang believes you are guilty of sabotaging the Christmas concert," Mrs. Holmes said.

Instead of denying it, Abby nodded. "Yes."

"Can you tell us what exactly you did?" Mrs. Holmes asked.

In a shaking voice, Abby said, "I stole all the concert decorations and hid them in the storage shed behind the mower because no one would use it in winter. I took Mrs. Center's sheet music and her baton she uses to conduct the choir. I also painted over the backdrop to ruin it. I — I wanted to get the concert canceled." She paused, looking down at her hands. "How did you know it was me?"

"You were the only one who could've done it," I said. "The music room was so cold on Friday because the window had been open, and it was still cracked open a little. When we looked at the window, the sill was wet, which made sense. But so was the floor under the window and under the table where you were working. That didn't make sense, unless the water was actually melted snow off your boots.

Your coat was damp too, even though you said you'd been inside all afternoon. But that wasn't true. You opened the window, climbed out, and took the stolen stuff to the shed in between Mr. Doyle's trips. Because it was the end of the day, and the shed is out back, no one saw you."

"What about Abby's footprints?" Rocket asked. "Why didn't that tip off Mr. Doyle that someone else was using the shed?"

"Oh! I know this one," Caleb said. "Abby walked

in Mr. Doyle's footprints, just like we did. It was windy and the snow was blowing everywhere, so Mr. Doyle didn't notice her footprints farther away from the shed."

"But why did you do it, Abby?" Tully asked. "You worked harder on those decorations than anybody else. You even have a solo in the concert!"

Abby hung her head.

"I'm so sorry. I like to sing, but I'm not very good. I was almost too scared to audition. When I got the solo, I was even more scared."

"What were you scared of?" I asked, but I had a sinking feeling I knew the answer.

"Being laughed at. I tried to back out. I went to Mrs. Center, but I was too scared to tell her I wanted to quit. I thought if the concert didn't happen, then I wouldn't have to sing, and no one would laugh at me."

"No one will laugh at you, Abby," Tully said.

"But Lyra is so much better than me. I'll sound awful next to her."

Then I felt terrible for how meanly I'd treated Abby. I hadn't thought about how Abby might feel. Not even a little.

"I made it worse," I said. "I wasn't very nice."

"It's still my fault," Abby said.

Mrs. Holmes rubbed Abby's shoulder.

"Thank you for taking responsibility."

"I'm really sorry," Abby said again.

Mrs. Holmes turned to us.

"Once again, you guys have impressed me mightily. Thank you so much. Now, I'm going to talk with Abby some more, but why don't you go tell Mrs. Center the good news? The Christmas concert must go on!"

"Yes ma'am!" we shouted together. Even though the rules were no running, we raced each other all the way to the art and music room.

Chapter Nine

Stealing the Show

The night of the concert, the gym was decked out like the most glamourous magical winter forest ever. Abby worked with Tully and Caleb to repaint the backdrop, and it was even better than before. Silver snowflakes spun and twirled from the ceiling and sparkled on the walls. The teachers strung white Christmas lights everywhere. It was glorious!

The gym was packed full of everybody's friends and family. Mom and Dad sat in the front row, grinning their best we-can't-believe-how-proud-we-are grins. When it was my turn to sing "Silent Night," I stepped out into the spotlight. The dragonflies were zooming around in my belly, but I concentrated on the music. I sang, and my voice was loud and pure. Each note seemed to soar out of me and float in the air. Even though I wasn't sure exactly what it meant, I was pretty sure I hit it all the way out of the park.

Then it was Abby's turn. I squeezed her hand.

"You'll do great," I whispered before Abby took the microphone. Abby smiled back at me nervously. At first her voice was soft and wobbly, but she picked up strength, and volume, and by the end, everyone gave her a huge round of applause.

Back in the choir, I kept singing, but I was thinking too. It felt good to be a great singer. But it almost felt even better to help Abby. She really did a great job. We both did.

It wasn't so bad sharing the spotlight with Abby. Third grade is big enough for two best singers, I thought to myself. Then I smiled the biggest smile of the whole night.

A Peek Inside Tully's Notebook

Scene of the crime: art and music room.
Snowflakes: Missing
Room: Freezing, when it should be warm.
Window: Open, when it should be closed.
Unexpected: Puddles on floor. Why?
Question: How can a coat be damp if it's
    been inside all afternoon?
Suspects: Travis the Terrible, Mrs. Collywobbles,
    Abby Campbell
Clues for Travis: Witnessed lurking near scene of
    the crime. Motive: angry at not getting solo.
Clues for Mrs. Collywobbles: Witnessed near
    the scene of the crime. Ponchos could hide
    stolen items. Overheard having a
    suspicious discussion. Motive: Quitting her
    job, keeping secrets.
Clues for Abby: At the scene of the crime.
    Puddles of water beneath her chair. Cold
    room. Damp coat. Motive: Afraid to sing in
    concert.

Q & A with Mr. Doyle

Lyra: How were you involved in the Christmas concert catastrophe?

Mr: Doyle: I wasn't involved. Not one bit. Not unless you count dragging giant bags of salt all over the school.

Lyra: Wasn't your shed used to hide the stolen snowflakes?

Mr. Doyle: I don't know anything about that. That shed door never closes right. With all the snow blowing around, it was hard to tell if someone had been in there.

Lyra: But what about the footprints? Why didn't you see unusual footprints around the shed?

Mr. Doyle: Because my footprints were already there, and sneaky Abby walked inside mine. Her feet were smaller, so she didn't make new tracks. I did go look at the ground right outside the art and music room window later. Sure enough, the snow was trampled and there were small footprints everywhere. The mystery could've been solved much earlier. It's all about knowing where to look.

Lyra: Thank you for all your help around the school, Mr. Doyle.

Mr. Doyle: Eh. Gotta get back to work now.

Writing Prompt
Write Your Own Mystery Story

There are several ingredients to include in a good mystery.

1. The mystery, which can be a secret, something unexplained, a crime, or something that goes missing.

2. Clues that lead to the real culprit.

3. "Red herrings", or distractions, that could be mistaken for a clue.

4. Suspects who might have done it.

5. The detective(s) who crack the case! Try creating a mystery out of a nursery rhyme. Did Humpty Dumpty really fall off the wall? Or did someone push him? Who would want to push him? Why?

Discussion Questions

1. Why was Lyra unhappy when Abby also got a solo part?

2. What were the clues that led the Gumshoe Gang to suspect Mrs. Collywobbles?

3. How did Lyra figure out that Abby was the culprit?

4. What was Abby's reason for wanting to cancel the concert?

5. What did Lyra learn at the end of the story?

Vocabulary

You may have noticed some of these words in the book. Do you know what they all mean? Try using each word in a sentence. Make flashcards with the definitions of each word and see how many you and your friends know.

audition	slump
blubber	snuggle
culprit	suspect
custodian	trudge
glare	witness

About the Author

Kyla Steinkraus loves mysteries and third graders (she happens to have one at home), so writing books for this series was a perfect fit. She and her two awesome kids love to snuggle up and read good books together. Kyla also loves playing games, laughing at funny jokes, and eating anything with chocolate in it.

About the Illustrator

I have always loved drawing from a very young age. While I was at school, most of my time was spent drawing comics and copying my favorite characters. With a portfolio under my arm, I started drawing comics for newspapers and fanzines. After I finished my studies I decided to try to make a living as a freelance illustrator... and here I am!